BEDLAM BUTCHERS

OFF LIMITS

ruby@katiwilde.com

ISBN-13: 978-1505311761

First Edition: December 2014
www.rubydixon.com

THE MOTORCYCLE CLUBS SERIES

The Death Lords MC by Ella Goode
The Bedlam Butchers MC by Ruby Dixon
The Hellfire Riders MC by Kati Wilde

More titles to be announced.

OFF LIMITS

THE BEDLAM BUTCHERS CLUB · BOOK 1

For Kati and Ella
I'd be completely lost without the two
of you. You are my muses!

OFF LIMITS

RUBY DIXON

ONE

"You coming with us to the panty raid tonight, Lucky?" Taco looks over at me from across the boxing hall and waggles his tongue in my direction.

"Bitch, please," I tell him, not bothered in the slightest by his lewd behavior. "I've got books to do before the fight on Friday night." I gesture with my pen from my small desk in the back of the gym. "So unless no one wants to make any money Friday, I need to work."

"Wouldn't mind seeing the color of your

panties," Taco tells me, unperturbed by the fact that I've just shot him down in the middle of the Meat Locker—the private gym and fight club owned by the Butchers.

His sparring partner, Colt, slams a fist into Taco's padded jaw. "Come on. If you want to get lucky tonight, you can't get Lucky." He grins, pleased at his own joke, and bounds on his feet, knocking his boxing gloves together impatiently. "You know she's bad mojo."

I roll my eyes. Took about five seconds for that to come up again. Figures.

In a club full of ridiculous names—like Taco, who likes to eat a lot of pussy, and Colt, who has an affinity for old guns—I'm called Lucky. And like a fat dude's called Tiny because he's not, I'm Lucky because I'm not. Lucky, that is.

I'm just about the unluckiest girl to ever grace the presence of the Bedlam Butchers, which is probably why I'm the club's kid sister and untouchable all at once. No one wants to flirt with Lucky, because they all remember the time that Lucky got Jerome sent off to jail. Or they remember how often Lucky gets pulled over for speeding tickets, out of all the people we know. They remember that Lucky dated Lenny a few weeks before Lenny got knocked off by the Eighty-Eight Henchmen. There was the ladies' club of biker babes that Lucky joined…for all of a week before they broke up due to infighting.

Lucky…isn't. And everyone knows it and gives me a wide berth.

It doesn't help that I'm Gemini's kid sister, either. One unlucky girl plus a brother that's one-half of the club presidency equals no getting lucky for Lucky.

I sigh and clench my thighs under the table as I do the books, trying not to think about how long it's been since I've had sex. At least two years. And vibes just aren't doing it for me anymore. I want a man on top of me, his scruff scraping my cheeks raw, his weight pressing me into the mattress, his cock pounding into me, his sweat dripping onto my skin. I can't get any of that good stuff from a vibe, just a cheap orgasm.

And I can't work if these guys are going to keep hanging around the Meat Locker while I'm trying to do the books. So I set my pen down. "Shouldn't you guys be leaving soon?" The boys are heading out for the annual Butchers panty raid. It's some sort of ridiculous rite where they designate a local bar and all the girls in town head over with a red thong to show that they're interested in getting laid. The club has a bunch of new sweetbutt for a few months, and eventually people settle down or wander away, and then it's time for the next panty raid. I'm never invited.

As if on cue, my brother Gem emerges from his office. "Five minutes, assholes," he tells the group. "Clear out." Of course, they all listen to my brother. When the prez says jump, you jump. Domino's two steps behind him, but he's the easy-going one. Everyone knows that if you want shit to get done, Gemini's the man you go to. Dom's the peacemaker.

The Butchers aren't like most clubs. Well, they are in that they like to drink, party, fuck anything moving, and get into trouble. But the Butchers are also a club that takes trust to the next level. They double up…in all ways. Even in bed. I've heard chicks love it—getting double-teamed by two of the good looking Butchers. I wouldn't know, considering my older brother Gem scares them all away from even looking at me. But the Butchers? They have two of every-thing—two presidents, two VPs, two secre-taries, you name it. Actually, I take that back. At the moment, they only have one treasurer—Solo, who's currently beating the snot out of a punching bag in the corner.

I eye him as the others flood into the showers.

Solo used to be called Joker, but then he and Panther—his co-treasurer—went off to serve in Afghanistan for two years. Doing their part, and all that. Except Solo came back with a limp, and Panther came back in a body bag. And laughing Joker's no longer a laughing sort.

He's fucking hot, though. I stare at his naked back dreamily. Sweat's running down tanned muscles. He's working out without a shirt on, and he's covered in tattoos up one arm and down the other. The big joker-with-machetes that's the club logo covers his broad shoulders, and it's clear he's in here working out very often. I've never seen him in the ring, but I'm guessing after Afghanistan, chicken-fighting with the local roosters loses a bit of its appeal. But his body is a work of sculpted art, and his hair is thick and brown, and he's got this incredible pair of sideburns that make me aroused just imagining how they'd feel on my skin.

Solo has an unlucky nickname like me. But his is because his partner and buddy, Panther, died. Solo is supposed to double-up with another one of the Butchers soon, someone to watch his back and handle things with him. But he hasn't yet, and hasn't in the last year, and it's pissing Gem off. He's tired of Solo being a solo act. Doesn't reflect well on the club and their standards.

Not that I'm allowed to be in the club, of course. I have a twat and therefore I'm only old lady material.

Which is a joke, considering that because my brother's Gem, no Butchers—paired or otherwise—are even going to give me the time of day. And no other club is going to look at me while my family leads the Butchers. Well, no other club worth having. I've been unlucky on that front, too. So like it or not, I'm Butcher property…but not quite part of the club.

Story of my life—lucky, lucky Lucky.

Solo's not heading to the panty raid, it looks like. He's still attacking the punching bag like it insulted his momma. He doesn't make a move as the others throw on their vests and head for the doors, laughing and joking and in an otherwise great mood. When you're in the club, you call it a 'cut' and not a jacket or a vest. I suppose because it's covered in patches and it means something then.

Me, I don't get anything because I'm the kid sister.

My brother Gemini winks at me. "Don't wait up."

"Don't worry," I call back, grinning.

"I want you to chain up the front, Lucky," my brother tells me. "You and Solo go out the back."

I give him a mock salute as I pick up the chains. Last year we had a break in and a rival club stole a ton of equipment, so we bolt everything down when we leave each night. The double-doors in front are easier to jimmy or to drive something through, so we make sure to chain those to stop most thieves. It's something I do most nights, and I wink at my brother as I follow him to the door. "Try not to nail everything moving, all right? Save some for Dom."

"No promises," he yells as he heads out the door, and I see Domino clap him on the back as the metal doors swing shut. Then it's just me and Solo alone in the Meat Locker. I run the chains through the door handles and put on the padlock, then return to my desk. Solo's there, still boxing. I step over closer to him. "Hey,

Solo? You'll need to go out the back tonight."

He grunts, and I suppose that's an acknowledgment to me. I watch him box a few minutes more, as oblivious to my presence as he was to everyone else's.

Then, I sigh and return to work.

Solo may have the official 'treasurer' title but since I have an accounting degree, I get most of the grunt work. I handle the payroll for the club and their activities, and I also monitor the bookings and tabs that are run up every Friday night fight. The books are given to me every Monday morning, full of scribbled notes and IOUs and it pretty much takes me all week to determine who was betting, who owes what, and who's paid up. The money never matches the book, so I have a week to get my ducks in a row before the next Friday…and then we do it all over again. I don't mind, though. It's almost like a puzzle, and I like puzzles. It also allows me to have a desk tucked away in a corner of the Meat Locker, and I like that. It makes me feel like I'm part of the club even though I have the whole 'twat' thing working against me.

I also like Solo, and doing the books lets me work closely with him, since he's the club treasurer and is responsible for collecting non-payments. Not that Solo would notice me anyhow... Lucky, right? No one wants any of Lucky's karma. Sigh. I bend my head low and get back to work, cataloging entries into a spreadsheet and cross-referencing them with the book and the awarded money.

I'm lost in numbers for some time when I hear a bang of the double doors at the front of the gym. My head jerks up and I frown at my surroundings. The few windows near the high ceiling of the gym are pitch black—it's late. The gym is full of shadows, and the only light is my tiny desk lamp. I hear the front doors bang again, and I turn off my computer monitor and my desk lamp, worry flicking through me, then slide off my shoes.

One of the Butchers would know the doors are chained after hours.

Then again, one of the Butchers would be at

the panty raid, tonight, unless they're hanging at home with their old ladies.

I tiptoe forward quietly, heading into the shadowy gym. Solo's no longer at the punching bag. He's no longer anywhere, in fact. I must have been too deep into the books to not notice him leaving, and another unhappy flutter starts in my chest. Who's out there? I cross the huge room, my bare feet silent on the concrete floor.

Someone bangs on the doors again, and they push open enough to make the chains taut. "Chained on the other side," an unfamiliar voice says. "Get the cutter. Her bike's still here."

Fuuuuuck. They're looking for me?

I tiptoe back to the boxing ring and crouch low, terrified. I don't know who'd be looking for me, but this can't be good news. I look around for a place to hide, but for a gym, we keep things pretty spartan. There's some equipment, the ring, Gem's office, and the showers. I should run out the back door and hope nobody's waiting there for me, but I don't know where Solo is. I peek over the side of the ring, my head barely visible

over it as the men on the other side push at
the door once more, and then a massive pair of
chain cutters are shoved through.

As the chains snap, strong hands grab me
around my waist and I'm dragged under the
ring-skirt.

I suck in a terrified breath—only to have
a sweaty hand pushed over my mouth. "Shhh,"
says a whisper-soft voice, and I realize it's Solo.
He lowers the skirt again, and then we're lying
underneath the ring in the oppressively still air
as boots clomp onto the concrete.

Someone's invading my brother's territory. And judging from the fact that Solo's here,
holding me in place while we hide? It's several
someones. My suspicions are confirmed when I
hear more and more feet enter. How many are
here? Five? Six? How did I not hear their bikes
pull up?

But I know that answer—I work at a gym
that's populated entirely by bikers. Mufflers and
the scream of engines are white noise to me now.

"Don't see no one here, Grass."

"Got to be here," drawled a too-familiar, horrifying voice. "I know the bitch works here at night."

A finger drags on my skin. I'm wearing a low-cut t-shirt that exposes a bit of cleavage and Solo traces a question-mark there.

I nod. I know who this is, now. And I want to cry.

I'm seriously so fucking unlucky.

Two weeks ago, I was feeling particularly lonely. It was the anniversary of Lenny's death and that always makes me moody. I went to a biker bar to get a few drinks and met a pretty cute guy named Grass. He seemed like kind of a wild child, and a little dangerous, but after several beers and contemplating my life of solitary servitude to the Butchers? He was looking pretty good. I even let him talk me into going back to his place. He'd taken me to a motel room (clue number one) and we'd gotten pretty hot and heavy until I pulled his shirt off and revealed his chest. It was covered in swastikas and the insignia for the Eighty-

Eight Henchmen, a rival club and some of the most dangerous white supremacists to ever ride a bike. I'd barely managed to hide my shock and suggested that Grass let me dash into the bathroom to handle a few 'girl' things. He did, and I'd snuck out the window, walking my bike a mile before daring to turn it on. I ran off into the night and never looked back.

I hadn't told anyone—especially not Gem—that I'd had a run in with the Eighty-Eight Henchmen. That I'd nearly fucked one in a desperate moment. That I'd run like a little girl. I figured that Grass was staying at a cheap-ass hotel, so he was just rolling through. I'd never run into him again.

Guess I was wrong.

Lucky's name holds true, it seems.

Solo's arm tightens around me, his hand clamping over my mouth again as boots stroll past, inches away from our heads. He doesn't have to worry about me yelling—I'm too frightened to even breathe, much less speak.

"That fucking cock tease has to be here

somewhere," Grass says. "I know that's her goddamn bike."

"Unless she's packing double with someone else for the night," another voice says.

A grunt. "Wouldn't surprise me. Little fucking whore."

"So what are we going to do for fun now?" another asks. "My dick needs to get wet."

I tremble all over. Grass and his friends showed up here to rape me? If they find me, will they even leave enough pieces for my brother to figure out what happened to me?

To my surprise, Solo's hand lifts from my mouth, and he begins to stroke my hair in a soothing motion. His mouth presses against my temple, and I realize he's trying to comfort me. He's trying to tell me that it'll be all right. That he's here.

But all I need is for one of the dumbass Henchmen to flip up the ring-skirt and realize we're hiding, and then I'm going to be gang-raped and murdered. Solo will be killed, too, and it'll be my fault. So I can't calm down.

"We could trash the place," someone suggests. "Or burn it to the ground."

"Fuck that," says Grass. "I want some action. Let's go find ourselves some pussy. We can pass it around like the Butchers do. Doesn't have to be Lucky, not tonight. Plenty of time to teach that cunt a lesson."

They laugh. I'm chilled to my core. Solo's hands are on me, his warm, sweaty scent in my nostrils, and I burrow against him, pressing my nose into the hollow of his throat. I might never get warm again.

I'm definitely going to have nightmares if I get out of this. So I squeeze my eyes closed and hate every moment of silence. I'm waiting for one of them to notice the ring, to notice what a good hiding place it is.

But they don't. One of them mimics a woman screaming, and the others laugh, and then the boots slowly move their way out of the gym. An infinite moment later, the doors slam shut.

Everything is silent.

I exhale a ragged breath. "Solo-"

His hand covers my mouth again, and he presses his lips to my ears. "This could be a set-up, Lucky. They might be out there, waiting for us to emerge. We need to stay put. And be silent."

Of course. I'm so stupid. I nod to let him know that I understand, and we continue to hide under the ring, waiting.

Minutes tick past. Solo's mouth is still close to my ear, and I feel his breath against my skin with every exhale. His other hand has slid to the flat of my belly, resting just above the waistband of my jeans. It feels good to lie against him. I've missed having someone to cuddle against when I'm sad or lonely.

Or hell, just to cuddle any time at all. No one wants to touch Lucky. I bet even Solo is regretting his time here at the gym with me tonight.

But even as I think this, his nose glides against my temple, and then he takes my earlobe between his teeth and nips it.

And I suck in a breath.

Did I imagine that? Solo's never shown interest in me before. Actually, he hasn't shown interest in much of anything since returning from Afghanistan. Maybe it's just his hormones charged up because he can't fight a six-pack of Henchmen. Two or three, sure. But there were more than that, and even the dumbest Butcher knows that there's safety in numbers.

That must be it, I tell myself as he licks and nibbles on my earlobe. It's adrenaline and he's forgotten who he's hiding with.

Even so, I'm secretly glad for his adrenaline, because Solo's mouth on my skin? God, it feels good. It's exactly what I need to forget about my dire predicament. The smell of his sweaty skin pressed to mine permeates the small area, and the air is stifling and growing warm thanks to our body heat. I don't care, though. I like Solo's damp skin, the hard muscle underneath, the scent of him pressing up against me. He's not wearing anything but a pair of gym shorts, I realize. He's lost his boxing gloves somewhere along the way—maybe they interrupted him while he was heading to the showers and he came to check on me.

It doesn't matter, really. All that matters is that Solo's next to me, and he's sucking on my sensitive, sensitive ear as if I'm sexy.

And God, I'm getting wet just from that small touch.

I bite my lip, not wanting to whimper out my desire. That would be bad in case someone is still listening. Maybe they didn't hear our furtive whispers earlier, but that doesn't mean they wouldn't hear them now. We have to be quiet.

Which means he should probably stop fucking my ear with his tongue.

Not that I want him to stop.

It's the best damn thing I've ever felt. Better than the time I screwed Lenny in the bed of his pick-up. Better than the time I got inducted to the Lady Killers (who quickly disbanded). Better than the sweetest chocolate. His tongue flicks against the shell of my ear and his teeth nip at my earlobe and I'm pretty sure my hips are bucking against the floor.

I hear a low, breathless chuckle against my ear, and I realize Solo's noticed that. Well now, that's embarrassing.

Or at least, it is for about two seconds, because his hand slides from my belly to the button of my jeans. He flicks it open and then tugs at my zipper, and the fabric of my jeans grows loose around my hips.

I inhale sharply through my nose. I should push him away. I really should.

But instead, my hand snakes up to those thick sideburns that make me so fucking wet, and I stroke his cheek. And oh God, they're bristly and rough and his jaw underneath is firm and it's the sexiest thing ever. I might come just from rubbing his jaw. His chin is clean-shaven, but his sideburns creep all the way down to the corners of his mouth. It should look old fashioned and ridiculous, but on him, it looks badass as hell.

He's still tonguing my ear, too, though he's

now migrating to pressing kisses on my neck occasionally. I don't mind this. I'd give up every inch of my flesh if he'd promise to kiss it and make it all better. His hand on my belly finds the waistband of my panties, and then he's pushing inside, to the curls of my pussy.

And they're wet. Wet, wet, wet. Wet because he's touching me and I'm aroused as fuck when I should be terrified.

He makes a low sound that I barely hear. He might be pleased. He might be laughing at me. I don't even know. I'm not entirely sure I care. Maybe he needs a hard yank after tonight's scare and I'm the only pussy available. Don't care. I'll take whatever he hands out, because right now, I'm feeling way too good to tell him to stop.

I bite my lip as his fingers push through my wet folds, and he strokes them up and down my drenched pussy. Those big fingers push at the entrance to my cunt, and then he's driving one inside me, and oh, sweet lord, his finger is big and thick and I want to ride it like a pony. A stuttering gasp escapes me despite my best efforts, and the next thing I know, he's kissing his way over to my mouth, and then his lips cover mine, even as he begins to thrust with his finger. His tongue pushes into my mouth and I welcome it. He tastes like sweat and man and all the things I've missed. I kiss him back fiercely, even as my hips start to ride his hand. His tongue begins to spear into my mouth in time with his fingers, and it's driving me fucking wild.

Then, his thumb finds my clit and my breath explodes against Solo's mouth. We devour each other as his thumb begins to flick a rhythm against my clit, even as his finger is buried inside me.

I cling to him, my fingers digging in to his shoulders as an orgasm blasts through me. I'm doing my best to stay quiet, but as I come, he begins to finger-fuck me again, and I'm so wet that I can hear each drive of his fingers into my quivering flesh. And I come for what feels like forever, and it feels fantastic. It's de-stressor and distraction all in one.

By the time my muscles unlock enough for me to sag against Solo's chest, he's nipping at my mouth with slow, languid kisses and his finger has stopped thrusting inside me. His hand's still in my panties, and it's wet, and I'm wet, and the fabric of my jeans is soaked.

And I feel so good I want to stretch and curl my toes all at once.

Solo's teeth glide along the line of my jaw and his hand slides free from its spot between my thighs. I smell my own musky release for a moment, and then I hear him licking his fingers, sucking my juices off of his hand.

And okay, that's pretty fucking hot, too.

I wonder if he's come. I didn't see any indication that he had, but maybe he's one of those still-waters-run-deep types that don't blink an eye as they shoot their load. There's one way to find out, though. I twist around in his grasp until I'm facing his chest and I reach between us and down to his shorts.

My hand encounters the biggest, hardest erection I've ever had gracing my palm. This time, I hear his breath hiss against my skin, and I know he wasn't expecting that.

Which, naturally, makes me want to do more. His shorts have an elastic waist, so it's nothing for me to push into them and into his boxers. And then I'm wrapping my fingers around the biggest, thickest cock I've ever had the pleasure of touching. He's scalding hot, and the fat crown of his dick is dripping pre-cum. I'm dying to taste him, so I drag the pads of my fingers over the head and then lift them to my mouth for a taste.

Musky and as delicious as I'd expected.

I must make a sound as I do that, because Solo's hand grabs my hand from my mouth and then he drags it back to his cock. He pushes his shorts down and now I have free rein to do what I want to him. So I roll my palm over the slick head until my hand is coated with his pre-cum, and then I begin to stroke him. He's so big my fingertips barely touch on the other side, which is exciting. I can only imagine what this monster in his pants looks like. It feels enormous.

I stroke him with quick, tight movements, and his face buries against my neck. We're utterly silent, though to me the air feels heavy with sex. I feel the tension in his body as his hips grind against my thigh, and his cock shuttles in and out of my hand. I squeeze him and change my motions, trying to get him to come as rough and wild as I did.

Solo's hand clasps mine and then he's helping me stroke him off, and I feel emboldened by the power I hold over him. His entire body is tense against mine. He strains against me, his cock pumping into my hand, and then he bites down on my shoulder. I swallow my gasp because it doesn't hurt as much as it surprises me, and then my hand is covered with hot semen, and he's coming all over our joined fingers.

It occurs to me that I have no idea what we're going to do with the semen coating our fingers since we're in hiding. I worry about it for all of a second before I decide to be bold and dirty. After all, I'm Lucky, and if this is all I'm going to get before the Henchmen knock me off, I want to experience everything. So I guide his fingers to my mouth and suck them clean, and then I suck my own clean.

And he's tense next to me, so I know he's one hundred percent aware of what I'm doing, and I bet he likes it.

Even if he doesn't, I don't care. This isn't going anywhere once we climb out of our hiding place. I can be as dirty as I want.

Now that we've made each other come, though, a lot of the tension seems to have gone. The gym is still utterly silent, and I lie in Solo's arms, wondering what he's thinking about.

Is he thinking about Panther? His buddy that died in Afghanistan? And how if we were doing a normal Butchers thing, he'd probably be nailing me at the moment while Solo held me? Or is he glad that he has me all to himself? Or is he wishing he wasn't here at all?

I'm lost in these thoughts for what feels like forever. Time passes endlessly slow in our hidey-hole, and things are now getting stifling.

Plus, the crotch of my jeans is damp from where I came, and I'm getting hungry. Not that these things compare to getting ganked by the Henchmen, so I'm quite happy to hide out a bit longer.

But maybe Solo's tired of being here with me. I feel his body tense, and then he pats my shoulder. "Stay here," he murmurs, and cool air floods in as he lifts the ring-skirt and crawls out. I press my fingers to my mouth, fully aware that they still smell of sex and cunt and semen, and do my best not to call out after him. I listen for sounds that will tell me that the Henchmen are still out there. That they're waiting on us to emerge from hiding so they can cut our throats… or worse. After incredibly long, tense moments of waiting, the skirt lifts again and Solo peers down at me. "Come on out. It's clear."

I emerge, a little stiff, and he offers me a hand to help me stand up. I take it, and pull my fingers from his as soon as I'm upright. I glance over at my desk, but working after all this seems stupid. On the opposite side of the gym, one of the doors is still hanging open, the chain dangling. "I need to let Gem know what happened here," I tell Solo. I'm not looking forward to that conversation.

He shakes his head and grabs my arm. "We're getting out of here. I don't want to risk those jackasses getting drunk and heading back here to see if you've returned."

"Makes sense," I tell him. "Thanks for your help."

"You're coming with me," he says. "They trashed your bike."

TWO

We re-lock up the gym as best we can and I grab my purse as Solo gets dressed and snags his keys. His bike was parked behind the dumpster, and I marvel at it for a moment. "Why's your bike here?"

"Heard them coming down the road and was the only thing I could think to do." He shrugs.

"You could have left."

He shoots a narrow-eyed gaze at me. "And leave you?" I feel warm for a moment before he adds, "Gem would kill me if anything happened to you."

Right. Because I'm kid sis to one of the prezs. Lucky me. I don't feel so lucky as he wheels his bike out and I gaze down at my broken little mama on the ground. Her tires are shredded and it looks like they attacked her chrome with the heavy bolt cutters they used to open the door. My poor bike.

"Leave it," Solo tells me. "In case they return. I'll give you a ride. Hop on."

Since I don't have any other options and I'm not about to stay here by myself, I do as he says. I climb onto the bitch seat of his bike and once I lock my arms around him, I start to tremble.

A delayed reaction to tonight's scare. The Henchmen were here, looking for me. If Solo hadn't been here, I'd have been gang raped and murdered. I start shaking like a leaf.

As if he knows what I'm thinking, he pats one of the hands I have wrapped around his waist. "I got you, Lucky."

Nice words, but no one's really 'got' me. No one wants me and my bad mojo. And then he starts his bike and there's no more talking.

As we drive, though, it's clear we're not heading to my apartment. I live across town in a little second-story condo of a place that Gem's partner Domino owns. He lets me live there for cheap rent, and in exchange, I do the payroll for the employees of the complex. But we're not heading in that direction—we're heading to the far end of town.

I can only speculate where we're headed, but my guess is that we're going to Solo's place. I've never been.

I try to picture what Solo's place looks like. He's kept to himself quite a bit since returning from the war, something my brother has speculated on more than once. I wonder if his home will look like a bunker of some kind, complete with sandbag barriers and guns everywhere and tell-tale signs of PTSD all over the place. Or if his place will be completely bare because he's going to leave us again. I don't know what to expect. Solo falls into the category of 'guys that give me wide berth' and what we've exchanged tonight is pretty much more than I've ever had with another member of the Butchers. Except Lenny, who was an initiate, but I got him killed before he could become patched.

It surprises me when we pull up to a tiny house with a manicured lawn. I guess maybe I was expecting an apartment in a shitty complex or something more 'guy' like. Every time I've gone home with a non-club guy, he's taken me to a shithole pad. I thought Solo would be the same, but he's downright domestic.

It's kinda cute. He's even got bushes and shit.

He parks his bike in the driveway and covers it with a tarp, then gestures we should go in the side door. I eye his house. It's a cute little 50's style bungalow that's had some improvements done. Not new and fancy, but older and kind of cozy. "I'm surprised you have a house," I tell him. I know a lot of full-patched members that don't do much more than ride their bikes and deliver pizzas, and crash on whatever couch will have them. This is all very grown up.

Solo gives me an odd look. His limp is more pronounced as we go up the three steps to the door, and I wonder if he hurt himself somehow, and I feel like an ass because I never even thought about it when I was climbing all over him.

"I saved a lot of my wages and my disability pay. Bought this at a foreclosure auction and been fixing it up. It's not perfect but it's mine."

Huh. No wonder my brother wants him as treasurer to the club. In his merry band of pizza delivery men, someone that's actually good with his own money stands out. Of course, I'm being unfair—lots of guys in the club have real jobs and stuff. It's just the ones that crash on my brother's couch are the ones I'm used to seeing.

He opens the door and waits for me to step inside, and I do. The interior is sweet and kind of homey. We step into the tiny kitchen and there's linoleum on the floor that's faded but clean. The counters are blue, the cupboards white, and there's even a backsplash with a fruit fresco. All of this makes me wonder if there's a Mrs. Solo somewhere in the picture that I wasn't aware of.

Oh shit. Did I just jerk off a guy with an old lady and not realize it? "Um, Solo, this is a weird question, but you're not seeing anyone, are you?"

He tosses his keys down on the counter and scowls at me. "Fuck, no. Why would you ask that?"

I point at the fruit fresco.

"Like I said, I'm still fixing it up. I didn't put that in there." He makes a face. "One of the bathrooms has wallpaper with the ugliest fucking roses you've ever seen."

I giggle at that, because it doesn't sound very manly at all.

"And call me Eric." He opens the fridge and pulls out a beer bottle and offers it to me. "Eric Smithfield."

Since we're offering real names instead of just road names, I guess I should do the same.

"Penny. Last name Taggert, just like Gem." I take the beer, use the hem of my shirt to twist off the cap, and take a chug. It's icy and delicious and oh God, I needed it. I don't realize how dry my throat is until I drink. I barely stop myself from choking down the entire thing in one swig.

Solo—Eric—is giving me a weird look.

I wipe my mouth, all self-conscious. "What?"

"Lucky…Penny?"

I flip him the bird. "Like I chose to be called Lucky." The name chose me.

He pulls out a beer for himself and then shuts the fridge. "I got a lot of questions for you, Lucky."

"That doesn't sound good."

"It's probably not."

He gestures we should go into the living room, and I head in that direction, my cold beer clutched tight. The living room of his house is sparsely decorated. There's a big framed poster of Mad Max on one wall, and a flat-screen TV on the other. A beat up green sofa faces the TV and a throw-rug covers hardwood flooring. The room looks pretty empty, though. I guess Solo's not so big on decorating. I sit on one end of the sofa and hold my beer since there's no end table to set it on.

And I wait.

He sits down on the other end of the couch and takes another sip of his beer, then rubs his forehead. "Should probably start with the obvious. Why were those guys looking for you tonight?"

The question's casual, of course, but I see his gaze slide over to me. He's wondering what sort of trouble I've gotten myself into. And I'm embarrassed to admit the truth, but I guess I've got no choice. "I picked up a guy a few weeks ago at a bar. We went back to a hotel room and I got a good look at his tats. He was one of the Eighty-Eight Henchmen. I snuck out and left him hanging." I grimace. "I guess he didn't like that too much."

"So now he's coming after you?"

"Seems like it," I say, and I don't know what to do with my hands so I start peeling at the label on my beer. "I never thought he'd take things so personally. Just more of my rotten luck, I guess."

"Did you tell him you were part of the Butchers?"

"No. We both know I'm not." Not really. Not in all the ways it counts.

"Still, he must have recognized you or your bike. Or something. He said you told him you work at the gym?"

I shook my head. I may be unlucky, but I'm not stupid. "I told him I'm a schoolteacher. So either he figured it out on his own or he's got someone watching me."

He grunts. "You know we're going to have to tell Gem and Dom?"

"Yeah, I know." I peel a strip from the bottle. "They're going to kill me."

"Nah," he says, voice softening. He looks over in my direction. "But they are going to want to protect you until shit blows over. It's not your fault you picked up the wrong guy at the bar." He takes another swig of his beer and then watches me again. "Why are you picking up guys at the bar? You don't date in the club?"

I can't look him in the eye. "No one in the club will have me." And it's not because I'm dying to belong to someone in the club...I just really want to belong. To have a place with everyone.

"Why do they call you 'Lucky' anyhow?" When I arch an eyebrow at him, he shrugs. "I was overseas. I don't remember you from before."

It might be the case. I shrug. I've come to terms with my...luck, such as it is. "Just lots of things, really. Jerome says I got him sent off to prison, even though Gem says it's not true."

"Jerome's your brother?"

I nod. "We got pulled over in my car when I was sixteen, and Jerome told me to act casual. I wasn't real good at acting casual." My smile is rueful. "They found a ton of heroin in my car with Jerome's fingerprints all over it, and when they pulled it out, I couldn't hide my shock. So Jerome went away for thirty years. Three strike law and all that." I toy with the bottle in my hands. "All because I have a shitty poker face."

"You're lucky he didn't get you sent away to juvie," Solo tells me.

"Yeah," I say flatly. There's that word again—lucky. "And then there was the time I dated Lenny. He and I dated for about six months a few years back. I thought he was going to make me his old lady. Turned out he had a lot of 'potential' old ladies on the side. We got into a big fight and I slashed one of his tires before I rode off." My mouth purses over the next part. "He stopped at a bar to get a drink, got into a fight with one of the Eighty-Eight, and they offed him. My fault, though, because he wouldn't have been at the bar if it wasn't for me."

"So how is that your fault?"

"Because we were dating, and I'm unlucky."

"I remember Lenny. He stuck his dick into anything moving. So are there a bunch of girls running around with the name of 'Lucky' now?"

I give him a look. It's clear he doesn't understand. "I'm just bad luck, Solo. You need to realize it…and probably keep your distance."

"Fuck that," he says, and pulls out his phone.

"What are you doing?"

"Calling your brother to tell him what happened," he says. "Go get yourself another beer."

I hesitate. Gem's going to be pissed as fuck. But I know Solo's just doing his job as a full-patched member of the Butchers, and I don't blame him. I don't move from the couch, either. Instead, I stare at Solo, waiting as the phone rings and rings. Just when I think it's about to flip to voicemail, Gem picks up.

"What?" I hear my brother's voice faintly through the phone. It's quickly followed by loud female moans and another male one, probably Dom.

Oh, eek. My brother and Dom are in the middle of having sex with someone. I blanch and race for Eric's kitchen. "Grab me another beer, too," he tells me, and then, to Gem, says, "It's Solo. We had some trouble tonight, man."

I'm a big chicken who's a little wigged out at the thought of hearing more of my older brother having a threesome with his best buddy and a random girl, so I hide in the kitchen while Solo talks to Gemini. I'm also a big chicken because I know Gem's going to be pissed as hell and I don't want to be around to hear the yelling. So I pull two beers out of Eric's fridge and then I poke around in his kitchen a bit longer, being nosy. Despite the girly decor, it's clear it's a man's kitchen. There's nothing but beer in the fridge and a bag of chips on the counter. He's got one sauce pan, two plates, and two coffee mugs that were clearly lifted from a local diner, seeing as how they have the logo. Total guy shit. His pantry is hilarious, because it's filled with ramen noodles and more chips. Hilarious, and kind of adorable.

I'm still being nosy and poking through his cupboard when he comes into the kitchen and tosses his phone down on the counter. "See anything you like?" he asks me, and there's a light note in his teasing voice that makes me relax a little. Maybe things aren't so bad.

"Oh yeah," I tell him. "If there's ever an

apocalypse, I know where to come for noodles."

Eric grins, and takes one of the beers from my hands. He doesn't look annoyed that I've been snooping.

"So," I say, since he's not volunteering information. "What did Gem say?"

"Said we'd meet in the morning and discuss what to do. He's busy at the moment."

"So I heard," I said, opening my new beer and grimacing. The girl he was fucking was making a lot of damn noise. "He didn't blow his top about the Henchmen?"

"He just wanted to make sure you were safe, number one. I told him I had you covered."

My face gets hot, because I think of what his hands were doing earlier. Parts of me were covered, all right. "Yeah. Thank you again."

"Don't thank me. You're a Bedlam Butcher, even if you don't have the patch."

That's...the nicest thing anyone's ever said to me. I get a little misty and stare pointedly at my beer as I drink. "So, is he sending someone to take me home?"

"Nope," Eric says, and his voice is a lazy, sexy drawl. "Said I'm to keep you in sight at all times until tomorrow morning. Late tomorrow, judging from things."

"Gee, I hope I didn't interrupt his booty call," I say sarcastically.

"You did. He was about to head over here to get you, but I calmed him down." Eric's watching me pointedly. There's an undercurrent between us, and I'm not sure what to read from his body language. "So you're fine with me for tonight."

"Oh," I say. "Sorry if I'm imposing."

He shakes his head. "Not an imposition in the slightest. In fact, it works perfectly with my plans."

And then Eric steps forward and hitches one finger into the belt loop of my jeans, and drags me closer to him.

Oh.

Just like that, my pulse goes wild again.

My lips are dry. "You have…plans?" God, why does my voice choose now to squeak?

"Yup," Eric says, and tugs me even closer.

"You sure you want to touch me?" I ask him. "I'm not very lucky for most people."

"Most people are idiots," he tells me. "I make my own luck."

"Gem know about this?"

"Don't see how it's any of Gem's business who I fuck," Eric tells me, and then he pulls me in for a hot, wet kiss that leaves me weak in the knees. His words are all talk, because we know it's Gem's business who we fuck. Gem runs the club, and the club comes first. But it's clear Eric doesn't want to deal with this tonight, and hell, neither do I.

Lucky just wants to get lucky, dammit.

So I fling my arms around his neck, all protests vanishing, and kiss him with all the pent-up passion I've been holding in. My tongue slicks against his and then we're going at each other, hot and eager, as if we didn't have a pet-down session not an hour ago. To be honest, it's only whetted my appetite for him, and I can still feel how slick I am between my legs. And I ache there. I need to be filled up, to be crammed full of his cock until I'm screaming out his name and scratching my claim onto his chest.

Eric seems to realize my eagerness, because he tears at my shirt, tugging it loose and then over my head. My bra is flung away with as much ferocity, and them he pushes me up against a wall, his hands going to my tits. He squeezes them as he kisses me again, and then his fingers tug at my nipples. My knees nearly buckle at the flood of sensations, and I brace myself against the wall before I can topple over because it feels so good.

"So, Penny," Eric breathes against my mouth, and his fingers continue to stroke my nipples until they feel hard as diamonds. "You want it slow and easy, or hot and dirty?"

Oh God. Choices, choices. "Hot and dirty," I tell him, and suck on his lower lip. My hand slides to the front of his pants and rubs against his hard cock. I definitely want it hot and dirty and fast. I don't think I can handle a languid bout of sex right now. My entire body feels primed as it is.

"Fuck yeah," he tells me, and gives my breasts another squeeze before he grabs me by the hips, hauls me onto his cock, and then presses me against the wall again.

I gasp at the sensation of his clothed cock pressing against my cunt. Even though there're layers of fabric separating us, I'm going fucking wild at the feel of him. My body's anticipating him sliding home, and I can't wait.

"You have gorgeous little tits," he tells me, giving them another squeeze to emphasize the compliment. "Makes a man want to stick his cock between them and ride you until I come on your face."

He's dirty talking to me, and oh God, it's sexy as fuck. I whimper, rocking against his hands, his cock, anything I can do to let him know I'm ready now-now-now. "Condom," I gasp.

"Bed first," he tells me, and his arms wrap around my waist and he carries me as if I weigh nothing. He pulls me into a nearby room and flings me down on the mattress.

As soon as he does, I'm scrambling to get out of my jeans and soaked panties. As soon as I toss them onto the floor, I realize he's getting undressed, too, though without the same urgency I show.

Fine then, he needs a bit of encouragement? I can do that. I watch him undress, and I bite my lip, then slide a hand between my thighs and begin to touch my clit. I'm so wet that as I rub, my flesh is making slick noises. His nostrils flare, and I can tell he likes the view. I open my legs wider so he can have more to appreciate.

He takes it for a different kind of invitation. He chucks his shorts and instead of climbing on top of me, he drops to his knees next to the bed and tugs my hips down toward him.

Then, he buries his face between my thighs, into my dripping cunt.

I cry out with pleasure as his mouth finds my clit. His tongue moves over it, circling like my fingers were, and my hands go to his hair, instead, so I can hold him there until I get off. It's not going to take much; my thighs are already trembling with each stroke of his tongue.

"Fuck, you taste good," he tells me, and it makes me even more aroused. "And you're so goddamn wet."

I want to tell him that I need this, need him, but I'm only capable of making incoherent little noises as he continues to suck and tease at my pussy. He licks the wet lips of my cunt and drags his mouth up and down. When he spears his tongue into the entrance of my cunt, though, I lose control. An orgasm blasts through my body, locking my muscles and tearing a scream from my throat.

"Goddamn, you are hot, Lucky," he tells me. He presses a kiss to my quivering flesh before getting to his feet and heading to a nearby nightstand. I watch in a daze as he pulls out a string of condoms, rips one off, and then tears it open. He smooths it on to the monster between his legs that I haven't even had the chance to put my mouth on yet, and then returns to the bed. "On your stomach," he tells me.

I obey, even though I'm boneless and quivering at this point. Sexy Jell-o. That's what I am. But I manage to flip over, and as soon as I do, he grabs my hips and hauls my ass into the air, then parts my knees. I obey, sinking down low onto the blankets and pressing my cheek there, so my ass raises into the air. My ass and my wet, wet cunt that needs to be filled up like, yesterday.

"Now that is one sweet view," Solo tells me, and his fingers glide over my spread pussy, slicking my juices everywhere and making me quiver uncontrollably. I'm still incredibly sensitive despite my recent orgasm, and I can feel another one is just on the cusp. I've always been extremely sensitive in bed, and I love a good multiple-orgasm. I'm hoping Solo realizes how primed I am and helps me along.

He sinks a finger—no, wait, maybe it's two—deep into my cunt and begins to pump them in and out. "Look how wet you are for me, Penny. You want my big thick cock in here? Filling up this sweet pussy of yours?"

"God, yes," I moan into the blankets. I'm

clenching around his stroking fingers, full of need again, just like that. "Please, Eric, I need to be fucked." I wiggle against his hand and spread my knees wider, trying to lift my ass into the air in supplication.

In response, he pulls his fingers from my sheath and spanks my ass with one wet hand. "That's what I like to hear, baby." One hand grips my hip, and I barely have time to beg for more of his hand when he fits the head of his cock at my entrance and then slams home.

And I give an undignified squeal. It's a mix of pleasure, pain, and delicious shock. It's been a while since I've had sex, and Solo's got big equipment. I'm wet as hell, but it's still a tight fit and it pinches for the first moment. Then, that delicious sensation of being utterly *filled* takes over and I moan with sheer pleasure.

"That's right," he murmurs. His hand slides over my ass and my lower back, and then he grips my hip again and thrusts fucking hard. Once. Then, he pulls almost all the way out and does it again, driving into me with such force that I slide across the blankets a few inches. And he doesn't stop.

And I love it. God, I love it. He's not being careful with me in the slightest, and I eat it up. I groan with every thudding stroke he pounds into my cunt, and he's moving so hard and fierce that his balls slap against my pussy as he fucks me, and that creates an entirely different set of sensations that drive me wild.

A few more thrusts, and I'm crying out his name, begging for another release. "Please!"

"Please what, Lucky? Please fuck this tight pussy of yours?" He rocks into me again, and his hand slaps my flank once more.

"Please make me come!"

"I thought you came against my mouth," he teases.

"Again," I demand. And since he's not listening to me, my hand goes to my pussy and I start to play with my clit as he continues to pound into my cunt.

"Nu-uh," he tells me. "That's mine tonight." And his hand pushes aside mine and he begins to finger my pussy even as he presses deeper into me.

I scream as another, harder orgasm sweeps over me. This one makes my entire pussy clench hard, rippling and tight around his cock, and I'm squeezing him hard even as every inch of my body feels squeezed with the fierce orgasm. "That's right," he murmurs between clenched teeth. "That's fucking right, Lucky. You're mine."

And he drives into me again before he loses control himself. I'm pretty sure my brains have been fucked into oblivion as his thrusts change to slow and ragged, and then he rolls both of us over onto our sides, spent and panting.

We're spooning and trying to recover our breath, but even as we do, his hand moves to my breast and clasps it possessively.

I am all his tonight, it seems. And I don't mind this in the slightest.

THREE

I WAKE UP THE NEXT MORNING TO A HARD cock pressed against my buttocks, and a hand sliding between my thighs. Solo wastes no time, it seems, because he moves straight for my clit and begins to tease it with his fingers. I moan and press back against him, and it only encourages him to move his fingers faster, driving me crazy.

"Hold that thought," he murmurs against my ear, and I make a noise of protest as his hand leaves my pussy. But then I hear the tear of a condom wrapper and he shifts behind me, and I know I'm about to get just what I need, and soon.

When he has the condom on, he pushes his hand back between my legs again, and slicks his fingers between my labia. "You wet for me, Penny?"

I nod and reach backward for him, running my hand along those sexy sideburns that drive me so freaking wild. They felt incredible against my thighs last night.

"Good," he murmurs, and he lifts one thigh and then pushes into me from behind. Then, we're joined, side by side, and he begins to rock slowly into me, his movements not as bone-jarring and intense as last night, but slow and delicious.

"Mmm," I murmur, loving the way he feels as he rocks into me over and over again, unhurried, as if he has all day to do nothing but sink into me and make me feel good. And I kind of like that thought. Of hours of endless pleasure, of his skin against mine, locked in sex...

But in the next moment, his hand steals toward my clit again, and he begins to rub it. All the languidness evaporates, and I begin to rock against his hand and his cock, unable to help myself. I'm moaning and arching and pushing against his fingers with every thrust, every tickling circle of his fingertips against my clit.

And I'm coming in mere moments, instead of the hours I anticipated. It feels so good I can't even be upset. Eric knows my body, just how I like to be touched, and he's making sure I come nice and hard before he gets his. By the time I start to come down from my orgasm, he clutches my hips and slams me down on his cock, and I feel his cock pulse inside me with the force of his orgasm. I smile to myself as his entire body seems to tighten against mine, and then he wraps his arms around me and buries his face against my neck for a long, long moment.

"Thanks," he murmurs.

My brows furrow. "Thanks?" What an odd thing to say. You don't thank a girl after you make her come. You thank her when she hands you a towel or fetches you a beer from the fridge.

"Was that the wrong thing to say?" Solo nuzzles my neck. "How about 'nice cunt'?"

I snort. "Try again."

"Good job?"

Now I'm just giggling. "You need to work on your pillow talk, Eric. I'm starting to see why you're single."

He caresses my arm. "I have my reasons."

Reasons for his pillow talk, or reasons why he's single? I fall silent and stare at the wall, blinking. I don't want to be the first one to move away, to get out of our cozy nest of skin and sex and blankets. In here, I'm safe and the world fades away. I think I could cheerfully hide for the next month or so and not give a damn.

But it doesn't last. Good things never do. Eric caresses my hip and then gives it a pat. "Since I'm a gentleman, I'll let you have the shower first. Then we need to go say hello to your brother and see what the battle plan is."

My stomach curdles. "Battle plan?"

"Yup," he says, and he rolls away, his cock

leaving my pussy and I feel all hollow and bereft. "The Eighty-Eight came after you. They're sure as fuck not going to get away with it."

SINCE WE'RE TRYING TO KEEP a low profile, we take Eric's Honda Accord to Crandall's Road-house, a favorite hangout of the Butchers. I tease him about how very normal his Grocery Getter is, since his bike is all ape-hangers and bobbed chrome. But he only smiles at me and puts a possessive hand on my thigh as he drives. And I like it.

It's almost like we're dating. Which I know isn't the case, since I'm unlucky and we've really only had a night of hard fucking, but I'll take what I can get.

We cruise to the Roadhouse, and park along the back, by the dumpsters. There's a ton of bikes up front, but the Roadhouse is well-known Butcher property, and I guess Solo doesn't want to take any chances. We head in through the back doors, and I notice that Solo holds them open for me, like a gentleman.

Man, I wish I could hook my claws into this guy permanently.

The kitchen staff ignores us as we head through; they know better than to complain at someone wearing the Butcher's cut, and Eric's got his on display. I don't have one, of course. We wend our way through the kitchen and into the main room of the Roadhouse. Crandall's is covered with license plates and bike memorabilia on the walls, so it doesn't immediately scream 'Butcher Territory'. But anyone walking in automatically knows it's 'our' place, just by the sheer amount of Butchers hanging out at the tables. Even though it's barely noon, every shadowy back booth is full, and a few of the round tables in the center of the room are occupied by old ladies and prospects. I belong to neither, and the sight of them makes me realize it every time. With a sigh, I hesitate, but Solo's hand on my back propels me forward, and we approach my brother and Dom.

Gemini and Domino take the booth at the very back of the Roadhouse. It's in the darkest, most private corner, and they always sit in the same spot every time. Sometimes I wonder what they could possibly talk about, but most of the time, I just don't want to know. Co-presidents, they've been friends since grade school and founded the club after serving a stint in Iraq together. Gem never tells me the reason as to why he insists everything in the Butchers is in pairs, but I'm sure there's a reason. My brother has lots of secrets.

Of course, he's not the only one in the family like that. It's just that mine tend to rear their ugly heads.

Solo steers me toward my older brother's table, and I see Gem seated in his usual spot, his dark blond hair slightly mussed. He looks sleepy. Must have been a wild night. Dom looks tired too, but he grins at the sight of me. He seems a little twitchy this morning. "Hey, baby girl."

"Hey Dom," I tell him.

My brother's never been as gregarious as his buddy. Dom usually hugs me as a greeting, and he acts more like my big brother than Gem does. But Gem? He tilts his head and studies me, and then crooks a finger, indicating that I should approach him. I do, and realize that I must be in deeper shit than I anticipated if neither Dom nor Gem is getting up to hug me or check that I'm okay.

I approach and Gem puts an arm out and gives me an awkward, sideways hug. "You good, Lucky?" Even though he's not getting up, his eyes are full of concern for me.

I nod. "I'm good. Solo saved my ass."

He nods and looks over at Solo. "Thanks for taking care of my sister."

"It's nothing." He crosses his arms and looks like he wants to say more, but remains silent.

Things are quiet for a long moment, and I frown, glancing back and forth between the men. Gem and Solo are staring at each other, and I can't read anyone's faces. My brother's arm is still loosely around my waist, but no one's speaking. Only Dom has that shit-eating grin on his handsome face. "Someone going to talk to me? Anyone?"

I look at Dom and his nostrils flare. His forehead seems a little shiny with sweat. Is he on something? I've never known Dom to take drugs. I look over at my brother, and to my surprise, he tilts his head back against the wooden booth and groans.

And then I hear a very feminine giggle come from under the table.

"Oh, fucking gross!" I yelp. "You have sweet-butt under there?" I scurry backward and out of my brother's grasp. Ew, ew, ew. My brother's getting a blowie while talking to me? Not that I haven't seen worse in the Roadhouse before, but does it have to happen while I'm three feet away?

"Not sweetbutt," Dom says, and that wild grin's still on his face. I notice he's not getting up either. "I'd introduce you to Kitty, but she's got her mouth full at the moment."

"Ugh," I tell him. Mouth and hands, I'd guess, since neither one of them is leaving the table.

Solo snorts with amusement. "I see you two

had a good night."

My brother just closes his eyes, a lazy smile on his face. "Great night," he says. "We're keeping Kitty, by the way."

Well, that's new. Dom and Gem usually love them and leave them. Kitty must be creative as fuck. "Greaat. As much as I'd love to meet the new old lady in law, can we talk about my problem so I can head to work?"

Gem opens his eyes and he frowns. "You're not working this week."

"What? Why not?"

"Cause I think we've got a snitch," Gem says to me.

"Snitches are bitches," chimes in the voice from under the table.

I roll my eyes, but both prez just laugh like it's adorable. God, she must be an incredible lay, then. I'll try not to hate her if she makes my too-serious brother smile. Gem needs more things to smile about in his life, and if this Kitty girl can bring him to his happy place, I'll fucking love the hell out of her. But first thing's first. "Snitch?" I ask.

Solo moves in and puts an arm around my shoulders. "Keep your voice low," he tells me, and nuzzles my ear.

He's clearly trying to make it seem like we're a couple, but I get all dazed and weak in the knees at his touch.

"Snitch," Gem says, and I realize he's been speaking in a low voice so it doesn't carry past his table. "You didn't tell anyone where you work, did you?"

I shake my head. I don't remember tons about that night, but I do know I gave my usual cover of being a schoolteacher. "Right," Gem says. "So someone shared that you'd be at the gym, and that you'd be working alone."

I realize he's right and I begin to tremble all over. Someone in the club hates me enough to sell me out to the Eighty-Eight? Jesus.

"I got you," Solo says against my ear, and he keeps me pulled against him, acting for all the world like a man nibbling on his old lady. "Ain't nobody gonna hurt you while I'm breathing," he tells me.

And I do feel better. My hand slides to his waist and I press my face against his neck. Funny how I fit just right against Solo. I peek over at my brother to see if he's noticing how cuddly we are, but he's got his eyes closed again, concentrating on whatever Kitty's magical mouth is doing under the table.

After a moment, Gem speaks again. "Way I see things," he says. "We tell everyone you're all hot and bothered about a new man, and that he's going to fight on Friday night. If this dick-face wants you, he'll try and make a move then." Gem opens his eyes and looks over at me. One of his hands slides under the table, maybe to stroke Kitty's hair.

I lick my lips. There are a few holes in this plan. "Whoever's pretending to be my new man is in for a fuckton of trouble."

"I can handle myself," Solo says.

Gem lifts his chin in a subtle nod, his only acknowledgment of Eric's words.

But this worries me. I like Solo. And I'm

horribly, horribly unlucky. I dig my fingers into his leather cut and shake my head. "You should probably stay away from me."

"No," Solo says at the same time Gem does.

I look back and forth between the men, frowning. "How is this all already decided?"

"Your brother and I talked last night," Solo says.

That must have been some talk. I shake my head again but Solo fists a hand in my hair and pulls my mouth toward his. "It's done, Lucky." And he kisses the hell out of me in front of my brother, which is both awkward and thrilling all at once.

I pull away reluctantly once the kiss is done, a little dazed. My mouth feels swollen from his claim. "So what now?"

"Now we wait for Friday night to roll around," Solo tells me. "And you're not leaving my side until then."

I stare up at him, wondering what this means. Not leaving his side at all for the entire week? Does that mean we're…sleeping together?

"You gonna kill Grass?" Gem asks.

"If I have to," Solo says. "He ain't gonna touch Lucky again."

And I'm chilled. This is all my fault. I'm the reason Jerome went to prison, and I think of Solo's handsome face behind bars, and my heart crumbles into tiny little pieces. "Wait, no—"

"This is club business," Dom says. He's usually the happy-go-lucky one, but his voice is serious, and I know what he says goes. "He fucked with club property, and now he's about to realize what it means to mess with the Butchers."

Gem nods, and Solo leads me away.

And I wonder if I'm the club property, or if Dom was referring to the gym.

I'm silent as we get back into Solo's car and head to my apartment building so I can get a few changes of clothing. Solo doesn't want me staying here this week, and so I guess I'm bunking down with him after all. I should be excited—an entire week of great sex!—but all

I can think of is the upcoming ring battle that Gem and Dom are going to leak to our snitch. Solo's in amazing shape and he's a good fighter, but I don't count on the Eighty-Eight to play fair.

And I don't want Solo going to prison just to protect me.

I notice as we drive that two bikes are leisurely following us, a few cars behind. I recognize the bikes of Toxic and Blade, the Sergeant at Arms duo for the Butchers. They're responsible for protecting club property from outside harm, and it looks like that's me at the moment. They fall back as Solo pulls into the parking lot.

"We have a tail?" I ask him, my voice dull.

"Just playing it safe, Lucky," he tells me, his voice smooth and unruffled. "Gem wants to make sure you're not jumped by anyone."

I nod and get out of the car. My apartment is on the second floor and I head up the stairs, ignoring the tremble of my legs. I'm unhappy with the way things are going. Poor Solo got stuck with me all because he happened to be in the gym late last night instead of going on the panty raid. I feel so guilty.

My apartment's untouched, which is good. I head in and grab a bag and pack a bunch of clothing in there, along with some overnight stuff. I don't say a word, though. My head's full of miserable thoughts.

"You okay?" Solo asks me. As I've been packing, he's scoped out my apartment, making sure everything's safe.

I say nothing.

"Now you going to ignore me, Penny?"

I look up and glare at him, then toss a shirt into my bag. "I'm not ignoring you, *Eric*. I'm just upset."

He looks baffled. "Why are you upset?"

"Because you're stuck in this," I tell him, shoving my favorite jeans into the bag next. "I'm shit luck, and I've rubbed off on you. You should have steered clear when you had the chance."

"You're kidding, right?"

I'm about ready to cry. I'm not kidding,

actually. I like Solo, a lot. And bad things happen to those I like. I'm terrified of what's going to go down this Friday night. What if the Eighty-Eight bring guns instead of boxing gloves and take him out? What if Solo murders him in the ring and there's an undercover cop? The potential for Bad Shit is enormous, and I'm freaking out.

He moves to my side and grabs my chin. "Look at me, Penny."

I do, and I'm surprised by the fierceness in his expression.

"You think I'm doing this because I'm stuck?"

"A little," I admit.

"You think I don't want to touch you? That I don't want to spend the next week fucking your pretty little brain out?" His thumb caresses my lower lip. "You think I don't want to toss you down on this bed right now and throw your ankles behind your ears and make you scream my name?"

I gasp. Liquid heat rushes through me at his words. Now he's not the only one that wants that. I want it, too.

His hand leaves my chin and slides down to the front of my shirt. I'm surprised when he grabs a handful of it and tugs it over my head, but I help him remove it. If this is leading to more sex, I'm all for that.

"You think I haven't been watching you every day for months?" Solo murmurs as he grabs my jeans and begins to unbuckle them. "You think I work out every day because I'm some sort of gym rat now that I'm back from the Middle East? You think I'm Solo because I miss Panther and not because I've had my eye on the prez's sister all this time?"

My jaw drops. "You have?"

His mouth twists into a wry grimace. "Everyone knows that Lucky's off limits. Gem doesn't want anyone fucking with her. So I stay back and I wait for my chance."

I'm stunned by this revelation, and by the fierce kiss he plants on me next. Then his hand is shoving into my panties, and he's rubbing his fingers against my clit in a rough, bold claim.

"Thing is, Lucky," he murmurs, rubbing this sexy, sinful sideburns against my face as he finger fucks me. My hand clasps his and my mouth is open in silent pleasure, because oh god, he feels good. "I'm tired of waiting," Solo tells me. "And I'm claiming you as mine. So if you don't want that, you'd better speak up now." And one thick forefinger slides over my throbbing, sensitive clit.

My knees buckle.

"Tell me what you want," he murmurs as he lays me down on my bed. "You want me to leave you alone? I will. I'll keep you safe this week, but I won't touch you."

"I want you to make me yours," I tell him, and my hands go to his face and I kiss him. I kiss him over and over again, and my tongue moves against his, and I feel the groan he makes as he crawls over me.

He unzips his pants and pulls a condom out of his wallet, tossing it down on the bed next to me. I eagerly shove my jeans and panties off my legs until I'm in nothing but my bra, and

I watch him as he rolls the condom on.

He's so stinking beautiful. "I want to wrap my legs around you," I tell him. Wrap them, and never let go.

Solo's eyes gleam as he looks at me, and he grabs my hips, dragging me to the edge of the bed. Then, he sinks in and I wrap my legs around him, just as I promised.

I hope I never have to let go.

FOUR

THE NEXT WEEK IS POSSIBLY THE BEST ONE OF my life. I mean, sure, I'm on the run from the Eighty-Eight and forced to hide out. I'm disrupting Solo's regular schedule, and I can't go in to work so someone has to bring me the books. And, okay, Solo's a shitty cook and also leaves the towels on the floor.

But I'm still having a blast.

I really like living with him. His cute little house needs plenty of stuff done to it, so I'm happy to help out if it means I'm less of a mooch.

I take over the cooking duties once Solo burns my breakfast, and we start to fall into an easy pattern. Sex in the morning. Breakfast. Shower and clean up. Work on the house a bit. Sex. Lunch. Work on the books. Sex. Dinner. Sex. Watch a movie together. End up having sex on the couch. Migrate to the bedroom. Sex. Sleep. Repeat.

I know it won't be like this constantly. Heck, I know it won't be like this longer than Friday. I guess that's why we're determined to keep our hands, mouths, and other body parts on the other person constantly.

Solo is all confidence about the fight on Friday. I watch him as he works out, and he tells me about the fight clubs they had while stationed in Afghanistan, the guys he's beaten, the street brawls he's gotten into. I don't think it's bragging as much as he's trying to convince me that everything will be fine. But when it's late at night and we're wrapped around each other, content, I worry.

God, do I worry. I worry that my bad luck's

going to catch up with me again.

Because I want more than just a few stolen days with Solo. I want to wake up with him, well, forever. Which might be silly and clingy and shit, but I don't care. When we go to bed at night, he holds me so tight that I'm almost convinced that he's thinking the same thing I am.

I guess we'll find out Friday night.

As I FIX MY HAIR in the mirror in Solo's tiny bathroom, he frowns at my reflection.

"What?" I snap. He's been eyeing my ass— and scowling—for the past fifteen minutes. It's starting to bug me. It's definitely making me edgy and I'm antsy enough as it is.

"You think your shorts are tight enough?" He scowls down at my ass.

"Seriously, Eric? I thought the point was to drive the Eighty-Eight nuts tonight. You think I'm going to do that in flannel pajamas?"

His mouth twitches, and I can tell he's trying to hide a grin. "You'd drive me nuts in flannel pajamas."

And then I can't help but smile. "And that's why I like sleeping with you."

"I just don't like the idea of all those assholes getting a good look at your sweet ass when you know it belongs to me," he says, and he comes up behind me and cups my butt like he owns it. "Half your ass cheek's practically hanging out the back here," he growls.

I ignore his manhandling and go back to curling the ends of my long brown hair. Truth is, my shorts are pretty damn skimpy. They lace up the front and have a low back and barely cover anything. I'm wearing them so I can seem like a slutty ho in front of any Eighty-Eight that show up, but making Solo all growly and possessive is a nice side-effect.

I've paired the top with a tight tank and a lacy red bra that peeks through in several spots, the straps visible at all times. And a pair of tall fuck-me boots, because they just make me feel sexy. I'm going all out with the hair and makeup, too. I've never looked so hot.

Kinda sad that I'm doing all this to bait some Eighty-Eights, but when I see the appreciative look in Solo's eyes, I have to admit to myself that it's not just for them.

"Guess we should go soon," Solo says, leaning against the door. "You get any hotter, this place is going to combust."

I grin at him, put down the curling iron, and give my lips one last touch of flavored gloss. "I'm ready."

"Let's do this," he tells me, and slides his cut over his shoulders. "You know the plan?"

I straighten his cut and smooth a hand over his patches like I'm his old lady or something. "Basically we sit in public, suck face and make a spectacle of ourselves. You boast about how good you are in the ring, and we hope to flush one of them out so you can give them the beat down, right?"

"Right."

I don't ask what will happen if they don't take the bait, or if something goes wrong. Solo prefers what he likes to call Occam's Razor—

the simplest way is usually the best. But me? I know my luck. I know if there's an opportunity for shit to hit the fan, it will. So as a Plan B, I have a small can of mace tucked under one breast in my overly-padded bra. Just in case.

WE CRUISE IN ON SOLO's bike. I'm on the bitch seat, and Toxic and Blade are riding just behind us in case we get into any trouble on the way in. But we don't, and we make it to the Meat Locker just in time for Friday Night Fights.

A speciality of the Bedlam Butchers, Friday Night Fights start promptly at midnight and go until dawn. I guess that'd make them Saturday Morning Fights, but it doesn't have the same ring to it. There're all kinds of illegal fighting that goes down, and clubs from states away, like the Hellfire Riders or even the occasional Death Lord. Basically, if there's a cross-club rivalry you want solved in the ring and feel like publicly beating the shit out of your enemy? You come to the Meat Locker. And while the Butchers make most of their books on plumbing gigs and shit like that, the real money's in the Friday Night Fights.

You'd think Gem and Dom would get into some shit with the cops over having a fight club, but rumor is that the chief's on the take. And since FNF goes on every week, it's a pretty sweet take. I do the books, so I know just how much money comes through.

It's not quite midnight, but there's already a sea of bikes in front of the Meat Locker. Maybe a hundred, maybe two. They're literally piled on top of each other, along the side of the road, and into the neighboring field (also owned by my brother). Gonna be a busy night tonight. I squelch the uneasiness in my stomach as I see a few bikes parked in the group with swastikas on them.

God, I hate the Eighty-Eight.

We head inside. It's hot as fuck due to the press of bodies, and smoky from cigars and pot and God knows what else. It's loud, too, and there's a crush of people, mostly men. Truth is, most old ladies don't head out for the FNF. I don't come often—Gem doesn't like it. Says I'm too young and innocent to see a guy get beat to death. Guess tonight's an exception.

As soon as we move in, Solo drapes an arm over my shoulders and we head for the front, where metal folding chairs have been set up ringside. All of the workout equipment that normally fills the space has been delegated to a back room, and folding chairs set up. There's a 'refreshment' table in the back that has beer, harder shit, and some really, really hard shit if you're in the mood for illegal substances. I look around to see if there are any Henchmen here, but it's too crowded to make out familiar faces.

"You want some refreshments, babe?" Solo asks me.

I shouldn't drink, but my throat is dry and I'm anxious as hell. "Beer?"

"Got it." He claims a chair in the front, kisses me long and hard in front of everyone, and then grins. "Be right back."

I'm left alone for a minute, and a little alarmed, but I'm surrounded by Butchers. Solo wouldn't have left me if it wasn't safe, so I'm good. My brother's nowhere to be seen, but Dom's sitting in a nearby metal chair with a curvy redhead on his lap. She's sucking on a lollipop and giving him lascivious looks.

At the sight of me, she bounds up from Dom's lap. "Hey! You must be Lucky. I'm Kitty." She grins at me. "And I suppose I should apologize for the way we met the other day, but your brother's too serious and I was trying to get a reaction out of him."

My mouth curves into a smile. It's only been a week and Kitty totally has him pegged. I see why they're keeping her. "Nice to meet you face to face."

She grins at me and twirls the pop against her lips, trying to seem casual. She sees my gaze on the lollipop. "I'd offer you a taste but I just blew your brother before we got here, and you probably don't want secondhand jizz from a relative." She winks.

"Well, that's a visual I could have gone without," I tell her.

She shrugs, clearly the happy and shame-
less type. I still like her. She puts an arm around
my waist and several guys catcall, obviously
thinking we're about to make out. But instead,
she whispers, "I'm supposed to tell you that the
guys are all packing heat tonight in case shit
gets bad. You're covered."

I blink. "Wow, thanks."

"No sweat," Kitty tells me, swats my ass, and
then prances back over to Dom, who's only too
happy to have her return to his lap.

Solo appears with two cold beers and I
beam at the sight of him. I still can't get over
how good looking he is. I really am lucky that
I get all his attention. He sits down and pats
his lap, and since we're on display tonight, I
straddle him, reverse cowgirl. It allows me to
press my butt right up against his dick. As if
this is something we do all the time, he hands
me a beer and wraps his other arm around my
waist. "Take the top off of mine, too, will ya?" he
asks.

I do, and hand it back to him.

"Perfect. Thanks, babe."

I sip my beer as his hand adjusts at my waist. Then, I realize as he pushes past the laces and the leather holding the waist of my shorts together that he's not interested in holding my waist. He's pushing his hand into my tight leather shorts, past my bikini panties, and his fingers slide against my pussy.

I gasp as he immediately brushes his fingers over my clit. We're in public. I'm two seats away from Domino, my brother's partner in crime, and their new old lady.

"You look like you're freaking the fuck out," Solo murmurs against my ear. "And you keep watching the crowd. Someone's going to think something's up. So I'm putting your focus back on me, babe."

And he strokes my clit. In front of everyone. It should be obvious to the world what he's doing to me. I'm sprawled on his lap and my clothes are tight and hide nothing. And I can't help that I'm getting wet as hell knowing that all these men are watching him manhandle me.

And maybe that makes me a pervert, but God, it feels good to be a perv.

"You're already wet," he murmurs. "I think you dig this."

I try to drink my beer, all casual like, but his fingers are working me over, and my nipples are tight and chafing with arousal. I lean back against him, biting back my moans as he manipulates my pussy and drinks his beer like no one's around us. Solo's totally casual. I can just imagine the conversation he'd have if someone decided to sit and chat. *What's up man, not much, just giving my girl a little pet and rub. Nice riding weather tomorrow, eh?*

And then Solo's fingers have found my slickness, and he's pushing deeper to wet them in my moisture, and brings his fingers back to my clit and continues to work it. And I close my eyes, doing my best not to start moaning and coming in front of everyone.

A bell rings.

In a daze, I watch as the lights go down and a spotlight flicks onto the center of the boxing ring. Like he's on TV or something, my brother swaggers into the center of the ring, looking lethal and dangerous.

"Welcome to Friday Night Fights," he drawls. His eyes scan the dark room. I know he can't see me or Solo because of the spotlight on him, but I'm a little humiliated that my lover has his hands down my pants in front of my brother. But Gem continues. "You guys know the rules. Shit's settled in the ring, and only in the ring. The fighters set the rules. You want to fight to the death? That's on your ass, not mine. Like every week, we take volunteers. You got beef with someone? Bring it here and let your boys bet on if you can hold your own. Here's how this works. We let the volunteers go first. Anyone that just wants to fight goes into a pool, and we draw names for match-ups. Once the fights are established, we take time to let everyone place bets. Then, we start. Any questions?"

Cheers meet my brother's stare. The crowd's hungry for a fight.

"Gonna take that as a no," Gem says. "All right, then. We got any volunteers tonight who need to settle a score?"

I tense in Solo's lap, half expecting him to jump up and offer himself. But he only continues to pet my clit, his hand moving in a big, circular motion that's going to get me off if he keeps doing that. I whimper quietly and clutch my beer as if it's a lifeline. As if Eric realizes how close I am, he pushes against my clit harder, determined to make me come by sheer force of will if nothing else.

It's someone else that enters the ring. A man hops up on the opposite side of the ring from us and enters the spot-lit area where my brother's standing and waiting. It's at that moment that my legs tremble and I can't take the petting any longer. I give a little muffled cry as I come, my legs jerking against Solo's as he presses a hot kiss to my neck and continues to rub the cascading pleasure through my body to extend my orgasm as long as possible.

The man in the ring, I see through a haze

of pleasure, is Grass. He's wearing the Eighty-Eight's familiar cut, and I see swastikas on his bare shoulders. He's handsome, so I guess I can see why I fell for his good looks—but there's a menacing glare on his face that makes me cold. He approaches Gemini and grabs the microphone from my brother.

"I got beef," he says with a growl. "Where's that fucker Solo? He's diddling what belongs to me."

I groan with embarrassment. Looks like everyone did see what we were up to. I know it's part of the plan, but I'm still mortified. Mostly because I just came, hard, and I'm soaked between my legs and probably all over Solo's hand from being 'diddled'.

Solo pats my ass. "Up, babe. Time to teach that shit a lesson."

I get up, trying to avoid eye contact with everyone since I know they're all staring. I adjust my shorts and tie them tight again, since Solo's hand has loosened my laces.

Grass is glaring in our direction in the

ring, so there's no hiding. Solo gives me a hard, possessive kiss, then climbs into the ring to face off against Grass. He stares him up and down as if he's a piece of shit, and I can practically feel the waves of distaste rolling off of Eric. Then, he deliberately licks his hand. "She tastes pretty damn good, bro—"

Grass snarls and lunges for Solo, and I gasp.

Gem steps in between them, and a few other Butchers join in the ring to keep control. Gem takes control of the mic again. "First fight of the night is between Grass and Solo. Eighty-Eight Henchmen versus the Bedlam Butchers. What'll it be, boys? Blood, breaks, or buried?"

He's asking them the rules. I suck in a breath, wondering what they'll choose. First blood? First broken bone? Or to the death? I don't want anyone dying over me—I just want to be left alone by the Eighty-Eight.

I hold my breath for even longer as Solo shrugs and gestures that it's Grass's choice. Please. Please. Please.

Grass's lip curls. "I ain't dying for any cunt."

He spits at Solo's feet. "Breaks."

"Breaks it is," Gem drawls.

"But if you want to sweeten the pot," Grass continues, his gaze locked on Solo. "You'll toss in the woman. Winner takes her home with him."

I hear Kitty gasp nearby, and my entire body goes cold. He's basically cornered Eric. If Eric says no, it's as if he doesn't trust that he'll win the fight. But if he says yes....there's a possibility I'll end up with Grass. My stomach recoils at the thought.

Solo looks out to me and waits.

He's going to let it be my decision. I press my hand to my lips. I don't want to decide. I don't want to be up for bids. But if I say no, Eric loses face. Do I trust him enough to put my body on the line for him? Do I trust him to pound the shit out of Grass? I'm usually not present for the fights. I don't know how good Eric is. I know he's toned, but I also know he's got a limp from A-stan that occasionally shows up when he's tired or hurting.

But…if I can't trust him to have my back, who can I trust?

Hoping I haven't sealed my fate, I nod.

A slow, delicious smile spreads across Solo's face, and I feel like I've made the right choice despite the terrifying wager. From the look on his face, he's utterly confident he can win; he just wanted me to be confident in him, too. "Lucky's up for grabs too, then," he tells my brother.

For a moment, Gemini looks like he wants to murder both of them. But he restrains himself. "Fine. That'll be our first match. Next up. Any other beef?"

Solo jumps out of the ring and heads back to my side as more men enter the ring, more bouts are scheduled. But I can only see Eric's smiling face in front of mine. And as he pulls me in for a hard kiss, I hope he pounds the shit out of Grass.

THE NEXT HOUR IS THE longest one of my life. We wait, and Solo keeps his arms wrapped around me as bids are placed and people bet on whether I'll walk out the door with Solo or with Grass. I want to find out what everyone's bidding on—if it's Solo or the enemy, but I'm afraid to find out the answer. What if I don't like it?

But then the lights go down, the bell clangs, and Solo hands me his cut. "Keep this safe for me, babe. I'll be back to pick it up in a bit."

"Okay," I tell him breathlessly, and clutch it to my chest.

He winks at me and then enters the ring, stripping his shirt off. He's utterly gorgeous. The spotlight makes hollows of his defined muscles, and his Butchers ink across his shoulders makes me proud. He looks like a rough boxer of old, especially with those maddening sideburns. Grass, on the other hand, looks puny in comparison. I'm sure I'm biased, and I'm sure I don't care.

Gem steps in the middle as the two men begin to circle. "First to a break wins the match. Ready?" He looks at Grass.

Grass nods, a sneer on his face.

Solo nods, too.

"Fight," Gem yells, and then backs out of the way.

Grass immediately comes in swinging. Solo ducks him and moves out of the way, his stance easy, his shoulders and body moving like a boxer. He's dancing circles around Grass, waiting for the other man to swing. And when he does, Solo makes it look like a joke. Grass lunges for him again, and again, Solo sways out of his reach.

Then, he turns, and quick as anything, he plants a bare fist into Grass's face.

The Henchman reels, blood spurting from his mouth, and everyone on the front row takes a collective step backward to avoid being spattered. Grass clings to the ropes, wipes his mouth, and turns around to go at Solo again. He lands a glancing hit, but Solo quickly shakes it off and keeps moving.

Hits are traded back and forth, but it's clear that Solo can run circles around Grass. The Henchman is fit, but Solo's built like a prizefighter and it's clear he's done this sort of thing before. My heart hammers as he decks Grass across the face, and the other man flies around and lands on the mat, hard. But then he gets up again, and the dance starts over. Swing, feint, hit, recover.

The next time he's down, Grass grabs at Solo's legs and manages to knock him off his feet. I gasp as Eric flies down to the mat, and then the men are tumbling together, hands flying. I barely know where to look as they roll across the mat.

But then Eric's sitting on top of Grass's chest, and he plows a fist into the man's face. Once, twice, three times. The third time, I hear something crack and blood sprays across the both the mat and Solo.

Grass screams in pain, and his hands go to his face. "You broke my fucking nose!"

"Good," Solo snarls. He gets off of the other man as Gem and the enforcers enter the ring. But instead of letting Grass go, he flips him over and grinds his face into the mat, and Grass screams again as his broken face is slammed hard against the ring again. "You touch Lucky again, and I'm going to break every goddamn bone in your body. You hear me?"

They pull him off before Grass can answer, but it's clear from Solo's body language that he means it. I'm breathless with excitement as he scans the audience, looking for my face. He's covered in blood and sweat and he's got bruises purpling on his face…

And I want to fuck the hell out of him.

He bounds down to my side and it's clear I'm not the only one on an adrenaline spike at the moment. I hold out his cut for him, but he ignores it and grabs me, instead. He drags me against him for a kiss, and his lip is split and he's bleeding and I totally don't care. I wrap a leg around him and he hikes me up around his hips and we could go at it right there and I wouldn't care.

"Gem's got an office, right? Cause I need to fuck you right about now."

"In the back," I pant. And I need to be

fucked, too.

People are whistling and slapping Solo on the back as we make out and stagger toward the back office. It's not an easy thing to do when the entire Meat Locker is full of bikers hopped up on all kinds of shit, but we manage to fumble to the back, and there's the door. Solo tries the handle. Locked. "Fuck," he snarls.

"Got a pressie from the pressies," calls a voice, and I look over Solo's shoulder to where Kitty is standing, a knowing grin on her face. She's dangling the keys from one hand. Then she winks and tosses them to me. "You're welcome."

I catch them and search the ring for the right key. My fingers are trembling with need, and Solo's hot body is pressing me up against the door, as if he's going to fuck me against it if I don't open the office ASAP. He just might.

But then the key turns in the lock and we fall inside. Gem's desk is covered in papers, and I hesitate. "Where—"

Solo slams the door shut and locks it. Then, he turns me and pushes me down on the desk, my belly on a stack of invoices. "Right fucking here, babe." His fingers rip at my shorts, and the laces fall apart again. Then, he's dragging them down my hips, and I barely have time to bite my lip before he's unbuckled his pants.

And then he shoves into me, hard and huge. I cry out because God, it feels incredible.

"You on the pill?" he asks hoarsely. When I nod, he slams into me again, and the papers on Gem's desk scatter. I cling to the edge of the desk, bracing myself for the next hard thrust.

My pussy's clenching hard at the rough treatment, but I'm loving it. "Fuck me hard, Eric," I pant.

He obliges, slamming into me again. "Never saw anything so fucking sexy as you, Lucky. You're all mine. You know that, right? I'm not letting you go. Not now, not ever."

I cry out as he continues to hammer into me and I want to agree—that I don't want him to let me go, but I'm coming already, primed from his earlier petting. My entire body shakes, and Solo grips my hips and continues to fuck me, hard, until I feel his cock pulse, and then he's coming inside me, and I feel warm and owned and exhausted.

He presses down on top of me, resting his sweaty skin against my body, his weight shoving against me on the desk. He's covering me entirely, and for a moment, all is calm.

All is awesome, actually.

"Think they'll leave me alone?" I murmur to Solo, not wanting to ruin things but I have to know.

"Pretty sure," he says, and then slides out of me. He grabs some tissue from my brother's desk and tries to clean me up.

I giggle, because it seems kind of ineffective. That, and I don't mind having his come wet between my legs. Maybe that's the perv in me again, but I love proof that I'm his.

"He's sure as shit not going to touch you once you're my old lady," Solo says.

My breath catches in my throat and I sit up on the desk and look at him. "You're making me your old lady?"

"Yes and no," he says. He leans in and kisses my mouth. "I need to talk to Dom and Gem first."

IT'S NEARLY SIX IN THE morning when the Meat Locker's finally emptied of the last partiers. It's been a good night for the books, and an even better night once the Henchmen were escorted out of the territory. Things are quiet and I can finally relax just a little.

Gem, Dom and Kitty are still hanging around, along with a few of the patched members to make sure no one returns to start up trouble. I've been clinging to Solo's arm all night, waiting for him to approach the presidents and see what they say. When Dom pulls Kitty into his lap and begins to lick at her neck while Gem watches with amusement, it seems like a good time. Solo gives my hand a squeeze and then draws me forward.

"Need to talk to you two," Solo says. "Bout my place in the club."

My eyes widen. Oh shit. Is Solo stepping

down as a Butcher? Everyone knows they fuck and fight in twos, and he's a party of one. He loves the club. I don't want him to give it up for me. "Eric—"

He raises a hand, quieting me. His gaze remains locked on Gem and Dom, and he has their undivided attention now. "Here's the thing. I need a partner if I'm going to continue on as treasurer. You know it, I know it, and I've put it off for long enough. And there's only one person I trust enough to take into my bed and to help me keep things running smoothly when it comes to the books. And she can't be a Butcher because she's Gem's sister."

I gasp. Is he asking them to make me a patched member? I look over at Gem, but he's expressionless. Dom, however, is grinning.

"Your sister does all the work of any patched member without the benefits," Solo continues. "And no one has the club closer to her heart than her. So if you want me to have a partner, I want her." He squeezes my hand. "And there's another benefit. If she's patched, ain't nobody in the Eighty-Eight or any other group gonna fuck with her ever again. They go after her now because she's fair game. I'm making her my old lady because I like her," he says, and gives me a smile that says volumes more. "But I want you to patch her because she's a Butcher through and through."

Gem and Dom exchange a look. Dom pats Kitty's ass and she bounds up and moves away, out of club business. I wonder for a moment if I should follow, but Solo's got a death-grip on my hand that tells me to stay.

"Here's the thing," Dom says, and he rubs his chin. "If it was just me, I'd have patched Lucky years ago. We ain't a misogynist club. Ain't nothing wrong with having lady Butchers. Hell, I think some of the guys would be down with it if they got to fuck alongside 'em. It's the little sister part that's the hairy bit." He looked over at Gem. My brother was still neutral, still stone-faced. "Some girls are happy just to be old ladies, but Lucky's never fit in with that crowd. And you're right that she does a ton more for the club than a lot of our patched guys do. So we'll put it to a vote at the next meeting and see what the others say. If they don't like it, it doesn't fly. If they're good with it, we patch ourselves a pussy."

Gem smacked Dom's shoulder. "Watch what you say about my sister."

Solo grins. "Thanks." He squeezes my hand again. "I'm going to take Lucky home now."

I give my brother a curious look as we turn to go, and to my surprise, he winks at me. A hint of a smile curves his mouth, and my heart thuds with excitement.

I'm as good as patched, now. He wouldn't be smiling if he knew it would turn out badly. And judging from the grin on Solo's face, he knows the same thing. The vote's just to make the others feel included.

I suddenly feel light as air. I'm about to be a member of the Bedlam Butchers in name, not just in action. And I'm about to be Solo's full time partner. When we head out to his bike, the sun's rising and the weather's gorgeous. I laugh at how beautiful the world is at the moment, and as we get to Solo's bike, he grabs me by the waist and kisses me again.

"You happy?" he asks.

"What, you can't tell from the grin on my face?"

"It's not official yet—"

"But it will be," I say, and I want to shower him with kisses. "Thank you, Solo."

"You'll need to get a new bike," he says. "We'll go shopping for one once we're sure everything's quiet and all clear. And you'll have to get your shit and move in with me."

"So you were serious about the old lady thing?" I ask him. It's still hard to believe. Me, the unluckiest woman alive, has had her luck turn around in spectacular ways.

"Of course I was," he tells me, and now he's frowning. "You think I'd lie about shit like that?"

"Well, no—"

He grabs a handful of my hair and pulls my mouth toward his. "Don't you know I'm in love with you, Lucky? Have been since I got back from Afghanistan and saw your pretty face. Gave me a reason to keep on even when I didn't feel like it."

"I love you, too," I tell him softly. And I kiss him back.

Because that's what the Bedlam Butchers do. They fight together, ride together, and they fuck together.

And I'm Solo's partner in all ways.

Welcome to THE CLUB

Ella, Ruby, and Kati love romance, love strong heroines, and love those oh-so-bad alpha heroes. We love stories that are hot, sexy, and dangerous. So when we got together to write this series, we only had one rule: to write the kind of romances that we love to read.

We also know how difficult it can be to carve out time for a full-length novel…and reading a book in parts isn't always as satisfying. Our series is written for the busy romance reader in mind. In each story, you'll find scorching heat, wild emotion, and a romance that will have you turning the last page with a happy sigh.

We're always adding new novellas to our series. To see a list of all available titles, please visit:

www.katiwilde.com

We always love to hear from readers! Please contact us anytime at kati@katiwilde.com, ella@katiwilde.com, or ruby@katiwilde.com. Or visit our Facebook page:

www.facebook.com/1theclub1

The Motorcycle Clubs series…for romance readers who want all the heat and emotion, but who don't have all of the time.

OFF LIMITS
THE BEDLAM BUTCHERS CLUB #1

Lucky…isn't. In fact, she's considered 'off limits' to the Bedlam Butchers because she's caused them nothing but bad luck in the past. As a bonus? She's also the president's kid sister. Single and lonely? That's Lucky's way of life. Now, the Eighty-Eight Henchmen are harassing her and they're out for blood.

Solo…is. In a club where pairing up with a brother to watch your back is mandatory, Solo still hasn't gotten over his partner's death two years ago. The club's pressuring him to name a second Treasurer, but he has to trust that person in bed and out. And it's damn hard for Solo to trust.

But when he rescues Lucky from the Eighty-Eight, maybe it's time for Solo to find a partner, and time for Lucky's luck to turn around…

PACKING DOUBLE
THE BEDLAM BUTCHERS CLUB #2

When Kitty hears about the notorious 'panty raid' happening at a bar Friday night, she heads in looking for a good time with no strings attached. She might want to get laid, but she does not want to be part of any motorcycle club's lifestyle. She's not good with following directions or taking orders, and she's been told that's what an old lady does.

But when she meets Gemini and Domino, everything changes. The dual presidents of the Bedlam Butchers, they stake their claim on Kitty and decide to show her what the club lifestyle is really about: riding free, living on the edge, and letting them show her just how good being claimed by two men can be. Kitty might like being the center of their attentions, but when her life takes a dangerous turn, she has to decide who to trust both in bed and out of it.

DOUBLE TROUBLE
THE BEDLAM BUTCHERS CLUB #3

In the world of motorcycle clubs, a snitch is a dead man. And the Bedlam Butchers have a snitch who's intent on taking down one of the newest members of their club.

Shy knows just who the snitch is, too–it's her older brother. But she can't do anything about it, because Shy's got no one to protect her. If she tells what she knows, her brother's going to sell her out to his new, dangerous buddies. If she keeps quiet, she's still at risk from the Butchers. She needs someone at her back. Enforcers Muscle and Beast are the perfect solution… if she has the guts to make a play.

But what's going to happen when they find out Shy has been withholding information?

WANTING IT ALL
THE HELLFIRE RIDERS CLUB #1

Saxon Gray is the one man I can never have, but the only one I crave...

Saxon Gray has reason to hate me. He spent five years in prison after saving me from a brutal violation at the hands of a rival motorcycle club – and he paid for that rescue with his freedom. I've never been able to settle the debt I owe him... until now.

The menace of that old rivalry is flaring up again, and as president of the Hellfire Riders, Saxon is the one man who can keep me safe. But I want more than his protection.

I want his heart.

TAKING IT ALL
THE HELLFIRE RIDERS CLUB #2

Heaven is finally having Saxon Gray in my arms. Hell is knowing that I might lose him.

After I spent years loving him from a distance, the president of the Hellfire Riders MC is finally mine. Every day he's at my side; every night he's in my bed. It would be everything I'd ever wanted, except my dad is sick, and trouble is brewing now that Saxon's club is taking over my father's. Because bad blood between the two MCs still lingers, and an old rule requiring Saxon to share me with the other club members is being used as a weapon, forcing him to choose between me and the Hellfire Riders.

And I don't know if he'll choose me…or how far I might go to keep him.

HAVING IT ALL
THE HELLFIRE RIDERS CLUB #3

Now that Jenny Erickson is mine, I've got everything I want. Until one shotgun blast almost rips it away…

As president of the Hellfire Riders, there's two things I care about: protecting my woman and destroying the Eighty-Eight before they take everything I've fought for. They've hurt Jenny before and I swore that I'd rip out my own heart before they hurt her again. Every heated touch, every scorching kiss is a promise to keep her safe.

Now the Eighty-Eight is coming for me—and no matter what it takes, I'm not going to let them lay a finger on her. I'll sacrifice anything to protect her. My freedom. My heart.

Even my life.

HIS WILD DESIRE
THE DEATH LORDS CLUB #1

I'm not supposed to want him, but I do.
I'm not supposed to need him, but I can't stop.
I'm not supposed to love him, but my heart won't listen.
Most of all? I'm definitely, under no circumstances, supposed to sleep with him.

Grant "Wrecker" Harrison spent three years of his life locked away. He's out and he's tired of hiding. He wants everyone, even his father Judge President of the Death Lords MC, to know she's his.

Chelsea Weaver loves Grant even though she knows its wrong. She knew it was wrong when she gave him her virginity and she knows it's still wrong three years later...because Grant's her step-brother and Judge is the only father she's ever known.

HER SECRET PLEASURE
THE DEATH LORDS CLUB #2

Pippa: I love two things–books and bad boys. I'm trying to kick the bad boy habit and hold on to the loving books one. When I take the new librarian position in Fortune, I immediately say yes when the Chief of Police asks me out and deliberately turn my back on the bad motorcycle riding boys that litter the Fortune landscape. After all, my bad boy yen was kick started by the frequent absences of my nomad father. But no one turns down a man like Judge, the president of the Death Lords MC, not even a girl trying to be good.

Judge: When Pippa Lang breezes into town in her little red convertible, the wind blowing out her big red hair, there is no way the dirty Chief of Police is going to keep her. That red hair belongs on my pillow and her hot body between my sheets. And no one, not the Chief, not the town, and not even Pippa, is going to stop that from happening.

THEIR PRIVATE NEED
THE DEATH LORDS CLUB #3

Annie: I've been the good girl too long. I don't drink, don't smoke, and live at home with my preacher father. The most daring thing I've ever done is work part-time at the library. Rule-breakers and lawless men aren't part of my world but not doing doesn't mean I haven't thought about it. And every fantasy I've ever had is promising to come true if I just take a chance.

Easy: The moment I laid eyes on Annie, I knew she was the one for me and Michigan. We've been partners ever since we served and now we do everything together. And by everything I mean riding, drinking, and women. If we can get Annie on board, it'll be perfect. Not only do I have to convince Annie, though, I need to convince Michigan, too.

Michigan: Easy seems to think sweet, delectable Annie's just going to fall into our laps. But my one experience with a preacher's daughter left me scarred—emotionally and physically. A good girl like Annie wants to experience a little danger but she doesn't want to live it and I'm not going all in unless this is for the long haul.

THE MOTORCYCLE CLUBS SERIES

The Death Lords MC by Ella Goode
The Bedlam Butchers MC by Ruby Dixon
The Hellfire Riders MC by Kati Wilde

Coming Soon

More titles to be announced.

PACKING DOUBLE
THE BEDLAM BUTCHERS · BOOK 2

ONE

"No way," I breathe, staring at the piece of
paper fluttering under the time clock. It's the
schedule for the next week of shifts at Chrome,
the bar I'd waitressed at for the last six months.
Even though we were always short-staffed on
weekends, I'd been marked off of Friday night's
schedule.

That isn't fair. Joleen knows I need tuition
money for the upcoming fall semester, and tips
are best on Friday nights. I've even specifically
requested to work anyone's overtime shifts. I
tell everyone I'm available every day, every hour,

because I have no social life other than school and work. I don't date—school has to come first.

So why mark me off Friday night? I need the money, and I always stay late to help out. I even dress a little extra sexy and put on my best flirt game to make a bit extra in tips. So what the fuck is this all about? I rip the schedule from the board and storm off to the cash office, full of indignation.

My boss is in the back room, cranking the coin sorter. "Joleen," I complain, and plop the schedule down in front of her. "I told you I need Fridays. Why am I off tomorrow? You only have two girls scheduled. That's not enough and you know it. Why—"

"Panty raid," Joleen says without looking up. "Bedlam Butchers."

"Huh?" I don't even know how to begin to reply to that.

"Tamra, honey," Joleen says, finishing with the coin sorter and turning around in her chair to look at me. "You're a sweet girl and a good waitress, but you can't work tomorrow night. It's a panty raid."

I ignore the fact that Joleen refuses to call

me Kitty. It's a little too tarty, she says to me. Fuck that. So I like attention. So I like men. I don't like being put into a corner and made to wear a label, that's for damn sure. As a former foster kid, I haven't had the best luck in life or ever had anyone to depend on. I suppose if anyone's a mother figure to me, it's Joleen. She's lived so much life that she can't help but have a few of the answers I'm seeking.

"I...I don't get it?" I tell her. "What's a panty raid?"

Joleen crosses her arms and gives me an exasperated look. "You're twenty two, right, honey?"

"Twenty four."

"Still too young."

"For what?"

"For the Butchers," she says. "Don't get me wrong, they're a strong club, and a young one, but I don't think you're their type."

What on earth is Joleen babbling about? "I don't understand anything that you're saying."

"That's because you're not in the Lifestyle."

The way she says it—all capital 'L' in there—makes me realize that it's a motorcycle club thing. Joleen herself dates patches, or so the rumors go. But Joleen is older than me and looks as if life has chewed her up and spit her out. She's unhappy more often than not, chain-smokes, worries about her bills far too much, and never dates longer than a week. I never see her with anyone permanent-like.

So if that's the Lifestyle, it's good that I avoid it. Chrome is a side-of-the-highway dive bar that gets its fair share of bikers, so I know not everyone has it as bad as Joleen does, but she's my best example...which is why I never date.

But the whole 'panty raid' thing keeps hitting a naughty bone, and I have to ask. "So...what's a panty raid?"

Joleen pulls out a cigarette and her favorite Zippo, lights her smoke, then indicates that I should sit down. I do eagerly, hefting myself backward onto a counter and letting my legs dangle.

"I'm guessing you're not a virgin, Tamra, honey."

I snort. "Not in the slightest."

"So, okay. Then I guess I can't shock you with this shit. A panty raid is when the boys decide they need a little booty around. A little more club sweetbutt, if you catch my drift."

I'm not quite getting what she's saying, but I don't want to derail her. "Go on."

"The boys pick out a bar and let the girls in the area know that there's gonna be a panty raid. The girls decide to show up, and the boys look for red thongs. If you're wearing one, that means you're interested in the club. If you're not, it just means you get panty-checked a lot that night. Lots of men, lots of groping."

I consider this. Part of me is appalled at the thought of men tugging at my jeans and panty-checking me all night, but the reckless side of is more than a little titillated. It's been a while since I've had sex, and while I have an entire freaking catalog of battery-powered boyfriends, they merely scratch the itch for a time.

And I've been itching a long, long while. "So what are the rules for the panty raid?"

Joleen quirks an over-penciled eyebrow at me. "Just that. Red thong means you're fair game."

"But....what if someone decides he likes me and I don't like him back?"

"Then I suggest you wear a color other than red." Joleen waves her cigarette. "Not that it matters. You ain't working, honey. Like I said, it's the Bedlam Butchers that are going to be crowding this place tomorrow night, and you're not familiar with the Lifestyle."

But...there'd probably be lots of tips to be made if I flash a bit of thong at them, and tuition is coming up. And heck, I like being a flirt. I bite my lip, thinking. "What if I said I wanted to work? That I could handle it?"

Joleen looks skeptical. "Now, Tamra, honey. I know you aren't the type to go hooking up with the patrons. You haven't since I hired you, and I like that you're choosy. But tomorrow night, you can't be choosy. Guys in a cut are different than the kind you might normally date. They don't like a tease."

"I can handle myself." Actually, the thought of a panty raid sounds pretty damn exciting.

"There might be some shit going down in the bar that regular people ain't gonna like seeing."

"I can still handle it."

"And your ass is gonna be grabbed three

ways to Sunday."

I grin. "Then it's a good thing I'm in the mood to get my ass grabbed. Come on, Joleen. Please?" I clasp my hands and park them under my chin in an attempt to look pathetic. "Pretty please?"

"You want to work tomorrow because it's a panty raid or because it's good tips? 'Cause the regular Friday night crowd ain't gonna be in, honey. It's gonna be bikers on the lookout for pussy."

"I'm aware. And I'll be careful. I promise."

With a sigh, Joleen parks her cigarette back between her lips and takes the schedule from the counter-top, then writes my name in.

I'm reluctant to go. There are so many things I want more answers to, and Joleen's just sitting there, smoking. So I idle a bit longer. "Joleen, can you tell me a bit more about the lifestyle?"

She snorts. "It's not something for a girl like you, Tamra."

"Why not?"

Her head tilts in an exasperated look. "Because you ask too many questions and you're not real good at following the rules," she says tartly. "You just do whatever the fuck you like and hope that your smile brings people around." And her words are mean but she's grinning like she's impressed.

I'm impressed, too. She'd pegged me pretty well. I'm not real good at things like 'listening' and 'obeying'. "So...bikers like girls that are sweet and all "yes sir" and "no sir"? Because that really, really doesn't sound like me."

"Bikers don't like it when their bitches lip back at them," she tells me. "The first time you disobey, you're gonna get a fist in the mouth, Tamra honey. Which is why you shouldn't go to this panty raid thing unless all you want is a quick bit of dick."

I've been celibate for so long that even a quick bit of dick sounds pretty damn good to me. "So basically, ride them for the night and then don't return their phone calls?"

Joleen's smile is mean. "Exactly, honey. Not unless you want a life of getting your old man a beer and sucking his dick whenever he wants."

I like sucking dick. And right now, I'm

a waitress at a bar that serves beer. So, you know, I want to argue this fact, but I know what Joleen means. These are the kinds of guys that don't respect what a woman has in her head, just what's between her legs and how it can make a man feel. "I get you," I tell Joleen. "One quick fuck and then out."

"Yup," she says.

Which, really, isn't a bad call. I'd be happy with a quick fuck as long as it's a good one.

THE NEXT NIGHT, I TAKE care dressing for work.

Normally, Chrome is a pretty low-key bar. I could wear jeans and the standard black work tank-top, and my wheel-shaped Chrome name-badge is the only decoration I need. If I want to dress things up, I'd wear some dangly jewelry and a few bracelets, and a bit of lipstick. Maybe a push-up bra.

Tonight, I am going all out, though. I'm either going to get spectacularly laid or spectacularly tipped. Maybe even both, if I play my cards right. I wear my best red lacy thong and a matching red and black bra. I have a short leather skirt that only goes to mid-thigh and has a slit that goes even higher, and I wear it with a pair of fuck-me black heels and my normal Chrome tank-top.

I pull my bright red hair into two loose pigtails at my nape and curl the ends so they bounce and dance against my pale skin. I put on my make-up with care, outlining my eyes with black and darkening my lashes until my blue eyes pop. The cherry on top is my mouth, painted a bright, inviting red.

I study my reflection in the mirror, thinking, hands on my hips. I look pretty damn good, if I say so myself. But what if there's no one sexy tonight? What if the bar is full of grizzled old men on dirty bikes and they chew tobacco and have bad teeth? I wrinkle my nose, thinking. After a moment of hesitation, I get out my biggest purse and throw in a pair of sneakers, jeans, and black granny panties in case I have a change of heart. Then, I toss the bag over my shoulder, ready for the night.

Bring on the panty raid.

Made in the USA
Las Vegas, NV
09 July 2023

74416357R00080